D1709909

A KITTY NAMED LITTLE BOY

BASED ON A TRUE STORY

by Ezra Turner
Illustrated by Dejon Simmons

Dedicated to
Debbie Lombardo

CONTENTS

KITTY

itty began what would be an eventful little life within a fenced-in yard where pottery was sold. Beautiful pottery in many sizes, colours and shapes filled this yard, which was close to a field where children could be seen and heard playing soccer after school and on weekends. Kitty and his siblings were born under a large shipping crate. This huge tan box served as the office for the pottery business and the space underneath it became Kitty's secure and snug house.

Kitty spent the first three months of his life curled up under the shipping crate alongside his sister and two brothers. The kittens huddled together to keep each other warm while they waited for their mother to return from the hunting trips she made several times each day to find food for herself. When she finally arrived back at their shelter, the kittens would scramble over each other to get her milk, which they craved and lived on. As they nursed, their mother would gently lick her kittens' faces and ears, making sure that her family was nice and clean.

Time passed and the kittens grew bigger and stronger. One by one, they began taking their first steps—that is, all except Kitty, who was the smallest of the litter. All Kitty ever wanted to do was snuggle with his mother, who took pains to offer him extra care. Yet however much she encouraged him to feed, Kitty usually got pushed aside by his stronger siblings. Many times he would go to sleep on an empty stomach.

One day Kitty's mother and siblings crawled out from under the shipping crate. Kitty watched and even tried to follow them but was too weak. He tried to cry out to his mother, but not a single meow came out and he could only look on as the last little tail vanished from sight. Kitty had never been alone before. He felt afraid and cold without the warmth and company of his siblings. He waited and waited for them to return but time ticked on and no one appeared, not even his mother.

Eventually, the sounds of the night began to filter under the shipping crate. The familiar lilting melody of the tree frogs' peep-peep-peep now sounded like thunder. Kitty could not imagine what had happened to his family.

When daylight finally came, he was still alone, still cold and now hungrier than he had ever been before. What was he to do? Finally, and with every bit of energy he could muster, he crawled out from under the shipping crate. At first, Kitty was blinded by the bright sunlight. Straining to see, he began to notice that the world outside his comfy house was strangely different. He looked left and right and all around, hoping he would see his mother and siblings come pitter-pattering towards him.

Instead of his family, Kitty saw something huge and unfamiliar lumbering around in front of him. Much later he would understand that this was Mrs. Lunn, the owner of the pottery business. She was busy moving pots around to make room for a new shipment and did not notice him. Of course, this could have been because upon seeing her he had shrunk back under the crate. From within its darkness, he watched Mrs. Lunn uneasily. Who was she? Had she harmed his family?

The next day, Kitty awakened to the sound of humming. It was Mrs. Lunn, who again was busily shifting her pottery. Feeling weaker and colder than ever, Kitty nervously peeped out from under his shelter. As he did, he looked up and right into the eyes of Mrs. Lunn, who must have heard the faint sound of his movement. Mrs. Lunn gently picked him up in her warm hands and cried, "You poor little thing!" Kitty was too weak even to squirm and simply gave a feeble meow.

Mrs. Lunn wrapped Kitty in a warm towel, then put him in a basket and placed a saucer of warm milk nearby. Noticing that Kitty seemed too weak to lap the milk, Mrs. Lunn put a little milk on her finger so he could lick it. And lick it he did! Before long, he was hungrily lapping the milk from the saucer. Mrs. Lunn gently began tickling Kitty's ears and scratching his head, just as his mother used to do. After he had finished every drop of the milk, Kitty looked around and saw that Mrs. Lunn was not watching him. Quick as a mouse, he scurried back under the crate.

By the next morning Kitty was hungry again. What should he do? He heard Mrs. Lunn moving about and inched to the entrance of his hidden place to have a peek. There, in front of his eyes, was a saucer filled with milk. He touched the milk with his tongue. It was warm and smelled sweet. He began to lap it up eagerly. Kitty even let Mrs. Lunn scratch his ears as he drank.

This routine went on for a couple of weeks. Kitty grew stronger and gradually lost his fear of Mrs. Lunn and the new world outside his home. Even so, he was careful not to venture too far from the container. He spent his days watching Mrs. Lunn go about her work and in fact became as attached to her as if she were his mother. After all, she did all the things his mother used to do for him!

After a while, Mrs. Lunn began inching the milk dish further away from the shipping crate, all the while calling, " Here Kitty, Kitty! Encouraged, Kitty wandered further afield and began exploring his surroundings. He discovered more and more places to hide. One morning Mrs. Lunn found him crawling out of one of her colourful pots! Afterwards, he leapt up onto her lap—as was his custom by now. Mrs. Lunn looked into his bright green eyes and smiled as she began smoothing his fluffy white fur. Kitty purred contentedly. This was his way of letting her know how much he was enjoying her touch.

Months went by and the Christmas season arrived. The pottery yard now bustled with strangers who appeared on a daily basis and seemed to be everywhere. Kitty regularly retreated to the peace and quiet of his shelter, where he hid until everyone had left. When the coast was clear, Mrs. Lunn would come looking for him, calling, "Here Little Boy! Here Little Boy." Now that Kitty was older and of course bigger, this was what Mrs. Lunn called him. Little Boy became Kitty's official name and the one he answered to.

LITTLE BOY
THE FOOTBALL PLAYER

One afternoon Mrs. Lunn glimpsed Little Boy sitting at the fence that separated the pottery yard from the field next to it. She noticed that he was intently watching a group of children as they played soccer. She was amused at how his eyes moved from left to right, following the ball as the children kicked it around.

Later that same day, Mrs Lunn left the pottery yard and after a while returned with a fuzzy little ball, which she dropped right in front of Little Boy. At first, Little Boy seemed afraid of the ball, perhaps because it rolled away whenever he tried to touch it. But in time he got used to this and would play with the ball every day! Whenever the ball slipped between the pots, he would use both paws to push it out! Little Boy became adept at dribbling the ball around the pottery yard.

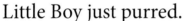

One day, while Little Boy was watching the children in the field kicking the ball back and forth, the ball rolled up to the fence. He grew excited and leapt through the open gate into the field and onto the ball. Feeling it roll around beneath him, Little Boy began hitting it from one paw to the other. "What!" yelled one of the children, "He's dribbling the ball!" At that, all the children ran over to watch the unlikely soccer player. "This little guy has talent," one of them cried.

Little Boy's moment of glory was cut short when Mrs. Lunn walked onto the field and picked him up. "You're a spunky one," she told him. "But you're just a cat and you're going to get hurt playing with these big boys." Little Boy just purred.

A STRANGER APPEARS

Not too long after the soccer field episode, Little Boy had another adventurous encounter. It happened one night when the moon was full and lighting up the deserted pottery yard with its glow. Little Boy was up and prowling around, but mostly amusing himself by playing hide-and-seek among the pots. He was darting in and out and in between them, as if hiding from the moon's rays, when he heard strange sounds coming from over by the fence. He looked in the direction of the noise and made out something climbing over the fence. Little Boy sat very still not making a sound.

Crouching between two large flower pots, Little Boy saw the intruder jump over the fence and begin strutting around the pottery yard. It was as if he owned the place! Little Boy noticed that the newcomer was black and had four legs and a tail just like him! Could it be that one of his long lost siblings was finally coming home? He watched and waited, hoping that the visitor might recognize him. But wait! The black cat didn't stop to greet him fondly but instead strode over to Little Boy's dish and began eating his food. Little Boy could not believe his eyes as he watched the cat greedily eat everything in his bowl.

Just then the black cat turned and saw Little Boy. The intruder's eyes were not friendly; they were fiery red and flashed angrily at Little Boy's green ones. Amazing even himself, Little Boy stood his ground. It was as if he were saying, "This is my home! And you're eating my food!" Finally the black cat jumped over the fence and disappeared into the night. Little Boy sat and stared into the darkness for a long time, wondering perhaps about this stranger that looked so much like him and yet stole his food.

When Mrs. Lunn arrived for work the next morning, she called for Little Boy as usual but got no response. Just as she was beginning to worry, she saw Little Boy slowly crawling out from under the shipping crate. She immediately sensed that something was wrong. "What's the matter Little Boy? Did something frighten you last night while you were here by yourself. I know you must get lonely," she said, placing his food in front of him.

When Little Boy wouldn't even touch his food, Mrs. Lunn got really worried and decided to take her little friend to the vet. "He's fine," said Dr. Benning. "But he has worms. This happens to kittens that spend time outdoors. I'll give him something to take care of those pests that can make a little guy seem mopey." By the time they got back to the pottery yard, Little Boy was already starting to get back to his playful self.

Mrs. Lunn was relieved and hugged Little Boy warmly. But she looked at him and thought that maybe she should take him home with her so this wouldn't happen again. But then she reminded herself that the pottery yard was what Little Boy knew. It was his home. Mrs. Lunn had an idea. She decided to go to the pet shop and find Little Boy a plaything. She returned with a little grey mouse. Little Boy recognized it immediately; after all, he had spent many nights trying to catch mice!

Mrs. Lunn dangled the toy mouse by the tail, swinging it from side to side. Little Boy stood on his hind legs and, with one swift pounce, grabbed the mouse from Mrs. Lunn. He squeezed it with his teeth. It squeaked just like a real mouse! Little Boy batted the mouse back and forth between his paws, toying with it as if it were a soccer ball. But after a while, when it never responded, he got bored and abandoned it.

That evening when Mrs. Lunn was locking up, Little Boy followed her to the gates of the pottery yard. It was as if he were trying to tell her that he wanted to go home with her. Little Boy watched Mrs. Lunn until she was out of sight and then went over to the fence to watch the children play soccer. He stayed there until the game was over, the ball was put away and the last child was leaving, walking away hand in hand with his parents.

Little Boy picked up his own ball and began batting it between his paws until he grew tired and felt hungry and thirsty. But he had no sooner gone over to his bowl to eat the food Mrs. Lunn had left for him than the black cat appeared in the pottery yard. This time the intruder arched his back and glared at Little Boy, as if ready for a fight. Little Boy wanted no part of that and ran towards his shipping crate. The black cat chased him and blocked his escape into the safety of his familiar shelter. But luckily, the bully stepped on Little Boy's toy mouse, which made a loud squeaking sound. This seemed to frighten the black cat, which turned and ran away. Little Boy then picked up his toy mouse and hurried under the shipping crate, where he stayed for the whole night.

The next day Mrs. Lunn noticed that once again Little Boy seemed out-of-sorts and not his usual lively self. Instead of helping her as she went about her chores, he lay around and ignored her. Finally Mrs. Lunn went over and picked him up. "What's the matter Little Boy?" she asked. "I wish you could tell me what's wrong." Then, as if thinking out loud, she said to herself, "Maybe I should take you home with me after all. I think it's time for that move."

HOME AT LAST

Mrs. Lunn's house was very strange to Little Boy. As soon as she released him from his travel crate, he darted from room to room, poking his head into every closet and corner. There wasn't a pot to be seen. And, he noticed, there wasn't another living thing in the house, not even a cat or mouse. It was clear that Mrs. Lunn lived alone—just like him!

Little Boy soon got used to his new home and in fact found it pretty cosy and safe. On cool nights he would jump into Mrs. Lunn's lap and cuddle up to her to keep warm while she watched TV in her preferred chair. In return, she would scratch behind his ears. Often on these occasions Mrs. Lunn would sigh contentedly while Little Boy would just purr.

When Christmas rolled around, as it did every year, Mrs. Lunn bought a tree and decided she would let Little Boy help her decorate it. He did this by dragging around the tinsel that just happened to be lying on the floor right next to him. Mrs. Lunn laughed as she watched him enjoy playing with the sparkly rope. After she had finished decorating and gone to bed, Little Boy expressed his pleasure still more by racing several times from the bottom of the Christmas tree to its very tip.

The next morning Mrs. Lunn came downstairs to find broken ornaments scattered all around the bottom of the Christmas tree. But instead of scolding Little Boy, she exclaimed, "I wasn't thinking of you at all! Let's start again!" This time Mrs. Lunn put the biggest, most colourful—and unbreakable—balls at the very bottom of the Christmas tree, right where Little Boy could reach them. In fact, Little Boy couldn't resist the temptation of them. He ran from one ornament to another, batting them between his paws as if he were back at the pottery yard playing soccer!

This was the beginning of many Christmases that Little Boy and Mrs Lunn would spend together. For as they say in fairy tales, they lived together happily ever after.

THE END

Made in United States
North Haven, CT
14 October 2021